THE CO~~DE BUSTERS~~ CLUB

TOP SECRET

FOR YOUR EYES ONLY

HANDBOOK

By Penny Warner
Author of the Award-Winning Code Busters Club Series

KEEP OUT

Secret File #1: Dossiers for the Code Busters Members

Dossier for Cody (Dakota) Jones

Code Name: "CodeRed"
Description:
  Hair: Red, curly, usually worn in a ponytail
  Eyes: Green
  Other: Freckles
Special Skills: Languages, reading faces and body language, surveillance, solving mysteries
Secret Message Hiding Place: Tree knothole in the front yard
Career Plan: Interpreter for UN or deaf people
Code Specialties: Sign Language, Pig Latin, Braille, Police Codes, Texting, Hieroglyphs

A note from Cody Jones

Hi, I'm Cody Jones. My real name is Dakota, but no one calls me that unless I'm in trouble. I look like my dad—he's tall and thin and has the same red hair, green eyes, and freckles as me. My little sister Tana—short for Montana—looks more like my mom. She's blonde, blue-eyed, and sturdy. Tana is deaf, so I learned sign language, which I taught it to the Code Busters.

My mom is a police officer in Berkeley and my dad is a lawyer. We moved here when my parents divorced. I missed my friends, but I've made new friends here, thanks to the Code Busters Club. I sort of have a cat—his name is Punkin—but I adopted him because I can't really have a cat since Tana is allergic. He really belongs to Skeleton Man across the street, but he spends most of his time in my yard. I made him a cool collar with his name in code on it. He's orange. That's why I call him Punkin.

Here's a secret message you can try to solve, using my favorite code, American Sign Language.

 Cody Jones

Secret Message from Cody in American Sign Language:

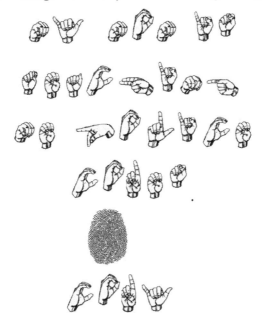

Dossier for Quinn Kee

Code Name: "Lock&Key"
Description:
    Hair: Black, spiky
    Eyes: Brown
    Other: Sunglasses, graphic t-shirts with cool logos
Special Skills: Video games, computer programming, military history
Secret Message Hiding Place: Doghouse
Career Plan: CIA cryptanalyst or video game designer
Code Specialties: Military Code, Morse Code, Computer Code, Washington Code, Pigpen Code

A note from Lock&Key

Hey, I'm Quinn, AKA Lock&Key. I started the Code Busters Club 'cause I like doing puzzles and codes and stuff. I'm good at math, probably because my parents are math professors at the University of California, Berkeley. I live across the street from Cody who's in the Code Busters Club. She's new at school this year, but she's cool. Skeleton Man is my next-door neighbor. We used to be creeped out about him but now because we know him better.

I like creating video games for the other club members to play, especially ones that have zombies and dragons and aliens and spies. I also like to make up new codes for the Code Busters to solve. And lately I've been doing origami—that's paper folding. I like to write messages on paper, then fold the paper into secret compartments. My bedroom is full of comic books, sci-fi stuff, and glow-in-the-dark stars on my ceiling that only shine at night.

My code name is Lock&Key. Get it? My last name is Kee, and the word "lock" is sort of like a mystery, and Lock&Key go together, so that's how I came up with it. That's about it for me. Gotta bounce. But here's a code to check out.

Secret Message from Quinn in Pigpen Code:

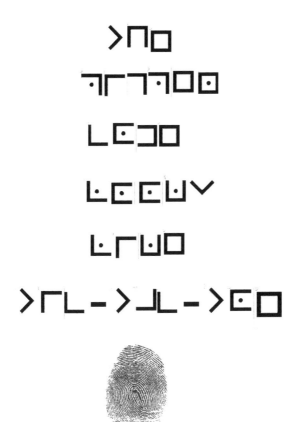

--.- ..- .. -. -.

Dossier for M.E. (Maria Elena) Esperanto

Code Name: "Em-me"
Description:

    Hair: Long, brown, usually straight but sometimes curled
    Eyes: Chocolate Brown
    Other: Fab clothes, sparkly accessories, awesome shoes
Special Skills: Handwriting analysis, art, fashionista, love animals
Secret Message Hiding Place: Flower box in the front yard
Career Plan: FBI handwriting analyst or veterinarian or fashion designer
Code Specialties: Spanish, hidden messages (Steganography), Semaphore and Flag Codes

A note from M.E

I'm M.E., which is pronounced "Em-me." It stands for my full name, Maria Elena. I come from a BIG family with three older brothers who tease me a lot, and a bunch of aunts and uncles and cousins. My mom is Mexican and my dad is part American Indian. I have brown hair and brown eyes. I speak Spanish at home with my parents, and English at school and with my friends, but I'm teaching the other Code Busters some Spanish.

My room is decorated with tons and tons of stuffed animals, because I love, love, love animals and hope to be a vet one day. I also LOVE clothes! Especially things with glitter and sparkles and sequins and stuff like that. I like to wear funny socks and cool shoes and colorful scarves and create my own outfits. If I don't end up being a vet, then I want to design clothes or be a handwriting analyst. That would be AWESOME!

I'm kind of a chicken when it comes to doing scary stuff—like sneaking into a burned out haunted house or meeting up with a mountain lion. But who wouldn't be scared about that, right?

Adios, I gotta go do my homework. See if you can crack my semaphore message below!

Secret Message from M.E. in Semaphore Code

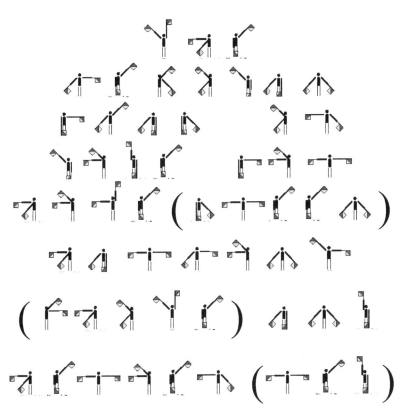

M E

Dossier for Luke LaVeau

Code Name: "Kuel-Dude"

Description:
    Hair: Black, curly, short
    Eyes: Dark brown
    Other: Saints cap, hoodie, Chuck Taylor Converse shoes
Special Skill: Extreme sports, skateboarding, motocross, biking, parkour
Message Center: Under Grandmere's porch step
Career Plan: Pro skater, stunt man, race car driver, professional athlete
Code Specialties: Crosswords, anagrams, wacky words, skater slang, pirate code, Cajun patois (a mixture of English and French)

A note from Kuel-Dude

Dude, I'm Luke LaVeau. I made up the nickname, "Kuel-Dude" because "Kuel" is an anagram of "Luke." And Kuel is Cool, right? I'm an only child—no brothers or sisters. I used to live in New Orleans with my parents, but now I live in Berkeley with my Grandmere. She's Cajun and says she's related to the pirate, Jean LaFitte. That means I'm part pirate! Awesome!

I'm pretty athletic and I love sports. I like to skateboard, bike, play basketball, football, do parkour, which is climbing up buildings and going around obstacles. People say nothing much scares me, and I guess that's true, except I don't like clowns. Dude, they're just weird.

My Grandmere loves puzzles, especially crossword puzzles. She makes puzzles for me using stuff from my homework, which makes it more fun, 'cause I don't like homework. She says if I don't do my homework, she'll mix up one of her potions and put a spell on me, but I know she's just teasing. She says she was a voodoo queen back in the day, but she doesn't scare me—except when she gives me the evil eye…

Anyway, that's it for me. Now, see if you can figure out the anagrams below. Later.

Secret Message from Luke in Anagram Code

Witer   a   gamesse

yb   giximn   pu

het   streetl

fo   ache   drow.

sIt'   nuf   dan   yesa!

DOCE   TRUSSEB   LURE!

|_ ( ) |< 3

Secret File #2 - Your Secret Dossier

Your Name: _____

Your Code Name: _____

Description:

    Hair: _____

    Eyes: _____

    Other Characteristics: _____

    _____

Special Skills: _____

SECRET Message Center: _____

Career Plan: _____

Code Specialties: _____

Your Photo:

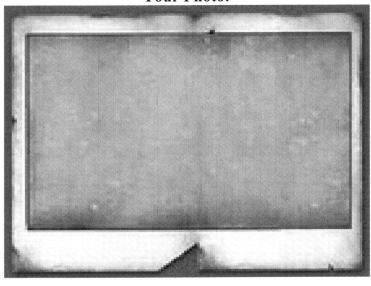

Your Fingerprints:

Left Hand	Right Hand

Pinkie_____   _____

Ring Finger_____   _____

Middle Finger_____   _____

Index Finger_____   _____

Thumb_____   _____

Secret File #3: CLUB RULES!
Form Your Own Code Busters Club!

The Code Busters have their own set of club rules, which include the following:

Motto: To solve puzzles, codes, and mysteries and keep the Code Busters Club secret!
Secret Sign: Interlocking index fingers (American Sign Language for "friend.")
Secret Password: Day of the week, said backward, ie. "Yadnom."
Secret Meeting Place: Code Busters Club Clubhouse in the eucalyptus forest.

How to set up your own Code Busters Club

1. First, gather up your members and have a meeting to decide on the details of the club.

2. Create a clubhouse. You can use a tree fort, a space in the garage, in the attic or basement, in a corner of the backyard, or anywhere, as long as it's safe.

3. Name the Club. Suggestions. Such as, Code Crackers Club, Code Kids Club, Top Secret Club, Eye Spy Club, Secret Agent Club, Crypto Club—or use "Code Busters Club."

4. Create rules for the Club. Such as, keep the club secret, attend all meetings, learn new codes to share with the group.

5. Determine the motto of the Club. Such as, to solve puzzles, codes, and mysteries, and keep the Code Busters Club secret!

6. Choose your code names. Such as, a word related to your real name, your name said backward, your name as an anagram.

7. Devise a secret sign. Such as, interlocking index fingers (ASL sign for "friend"), special handshake, or secret gesture.

8. Create a secret password. Such as, day of the week said backward, like "yadnom," initials tapped in Morse Code, special coded word.

9. Gather your Code Busting supplies. Such as, backpacks, notebooks, pens, flashlights, magnifying glasses, disguises, maps, spy stuff, detective kit, and so on.

Secret File #4:

How to Disguise Your SECRET MESSAGES

1. Get a 12-inch by 12-inch sheet of scrapbook paper.

2. Print side down, fold into thirds, at 4 inches and 8 inches.

3. Turn 90 degrees and fold again into thirds, at 4 and 8 inches.

4. Fold each corner in half, inward.

5. Turn paper over and fold squares from left to right.

6. Turn paper over, hold ends of opposite corners, push in gently to form square in center.

7. Fold down one triangle, fold down the next one on the left, fold down the next one on the left, then fold the fourth triangle and tuck the tip into the fold of the first triangle.

Secret File #5: Crack the SECRET CODES

These codes are *top secret*, used by the Code Busters. Use them to write secret messages.
Underneath are some coded secret messages for you to solve using your Code Buster Cards.

1. Alpha-Numeric Code

25-15-21   3-1-14   1-12-19-15   23-18-9-20-5

20-8-5   14-21-13-2-5-18-19   9-14   18-5-22-5-18-19-5.

2. American Sign Language

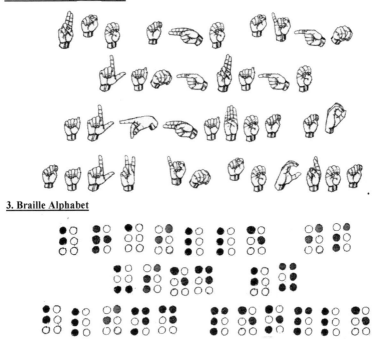

3. Braille Alphabet

8-19-4   1-16-4-7-16-9   1-11-23-19-4-9

25-19-4-4-13   11-7   21-6-12   8-2   6-7-4 !

5. Egyptian Hieroglyphic Code

6. Flag Code

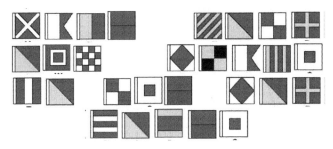

7. Phonetic Alphabet Code

PAPA HOTEL OSCAR NOVEMBER ECHO TANGO INDIA CHARLIE

ALPHA LIMA PAPA HOTEL ALPHA BRAVO ECHO TANGO

INDIA SIERRA   UNIFORM SIERRA ECHO DELTA   BRAVO YANKEE

MIKE INDIA LIMA INDIA TANGO ALPHA ROMEO YANKEE

8. Pigpen Code

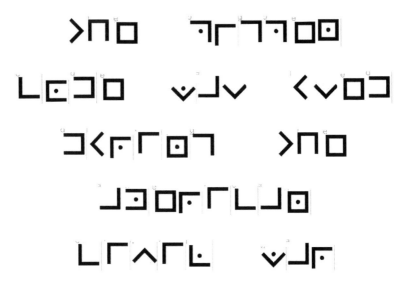

9. Pirate Code

Ahoy, Bucko!

Gangway for the blaggard who's been pillaging booty and grub.

We'll keelhaul the addled thief by sending him to Davy Jones' Locker!

Belay and fair winds!

10. Reverse Alphabet Code

Gsv ivevihv zlkszyvg rh lmv lu gsv vzhrvhg xlwvh.

11. Semaphore Code

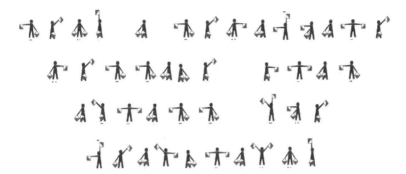

12. Texting Code

Hey, BFF!   S'UP GRL?

C U L8R 4 Whatev.   LOL.   B4N.   XOXO.

13. Vowel-less Code

SNDTTHLTTRSTCRCKTHCD.

More Activities Using Codes

1. Write a note to your friend in your favorite code.
2. Write your plans for your own Code Busters Club in another code.
3. Write a list of supplies you need for your Code Busters Club in another code.

How to Create Your Own Secret Codes

1. Draw simple little pictures for each alphabet letter.
2. Use computer symbols and type them next to the alphabet letters.
3. Substitute the names of animals, foods, people, or other categories for each letter.
4. Make up your own creative symbols for each letter.
5. Be inventive with the alphabet letters and change them into designs.
6. Write the top parts of each letter on one side, the bottom on the other, and put them together.

Secret File #6: How to Tell if You're a *Real* CODE BUSTER

Take this quiz to see if you're ready to be a *real* Code Buster!

1. English is your second language. Your first language is Pig Latin.
2. When you meet someone, you ask for their code name instead of their real name.
3. You do your homework in invisible ink.
4. All of your book reports are encrypted.
5. You wear night goggles to bed so you can see in the dark.
6. You call your fellow Code Busters "operatives."
7. You can tap out any song in Morse Code.
8. You prefer to type your homework on the Enigma machine rather than the computer.
9. You have the blueprints to your school and know where the secret passageways are.
10. Your cell phone is a language translator, magnifying glass, walkie-talkie, and flashlight.
11. You've translated the entire FBI handbook into Hieroglyphs.
12. You wear a disguise when sent to the principal's office.
13. You think your parents may be double agents.
14. You suspect the school bully is actually a mole.
15. Your dog is equipped with a surveillance camera.
16. You think the formula for invisible ink is the greatest invention in the world.
17. You cell phone number is code for "SAF-LINE."
18. Your mailbox is a "dead drop."
19. When you go to camp, you're "off the grid."
20. When asked a question, you answer, "The fox is in the henhouse."
21. Your watch is equipped with a hidden camera.
22. Your lunchbox has a tracking device in case it's ever stolen.
23. Your bedroom is blocked off with Crime Scene tape.
24. All of your homework is marked "Top Secret."
25. Your middle name is confidential.
26. When mailing a coded letter, you hide the decoder key under the stamp.
27. You give your home address in latitude and longitude.
28. You'd rather go to Quantico than Disneyland.
29. You eat edible paper with coded messages for breakfast.
30. Your BFF wrote "SOS-CU@1300@HQ" and you know what that means.
31. Your comic books are full of eyeholes so you can spy on people.
32. You have cell phone apps for a police siren, a scream, a fake Taser, and the theme song from Scooby Doo.

Secret File #7: How to Make INVISIBLE INK

There are lots of ways to make your own invisible ink. Try each of these to see which one you like the best.

1. Lemon Juice

    Write your message with lemon juice, using a Q-tip on plain white paper. Let it dry, then send it to a friend and have them hold it over a lightbulb.

2. Milk

    Instead of lemon juice, use milk. Follow the instructions above.

3. Baking Soda

    Mix a few spoonfuls of baking soda with water to make a paste. Use a Q-tip to write your message. To read the message, hold the paper over a lightbulb or dip a Q-tip in grape juice and rub it over the paper.

4. White Crayon

    Write a message on white paper with a white crayon. Have your friend color over the paper with a marker to see the secret message.

5. Banana

    Write a message on a banana peel with a toothpick. About an hour later, the message will magically appear.

Secret File #8: How to Type INVISIBLE MESSAGES

You can send an invisible message to a friend using the computer. Just follow these instructions.

1. Type your message in an email using a favorite font using the black color.

2. Highlight/select the message when you're finished.

3. Go to fonts and click on the **white**/clear color. Your message will disappear!

4. Email the message to your friend and tell him or her to highlight/select the message area, then go to fonts and click on the **black** color.

5. Voila! The message magically appears!

Secret File #9: Meet the Author

Who is PENNY WARNER?

Hi! I'm Penny Warner, author of the **CODE BUSTERS CLUB** series, as well as about sixty other books, mostly fun things to do with kids—snacks to eat, games to play, birthdays to celebrate. I love to make up stuff, especially for kids, and I love mysteries, especially Nancy Drew, Agatha Christie, and Sherlock Holmes. I even wrote a book about Nancy Drew called **THE OFFICIAL NANCY DREW HANDBOOK**.

I love writing the Code Busters Club series because I love creating and cracking codes. When I was a kid, I learned Sign Language, Morse code, Pig Latin and a bunch of other fun codes, so I could send secret messages to my friends. After I got my degrees in Child Development and Special Education (I teach Child Development at the local college), I wrote a bunch of activity books for kids and mysteries for adults. That's when I thought it would be fun to write a mystery for kids filled with codes for readers to solve!

When I'm not writing books or teaching classes, I like creating mysteries games for libraries so they can raise money for more books, and visiting schools where I present Code Buster Club events based on my books. The Code Busters Club books are published in Japan, Brazil, and Turkey, in case you can read other languages.

Do you have all of the Code Busters Club Books?

Book #1 - THE CODE BUSTERS CLUB: SECRET OF THE SKELETON KEY
Agatha Award Finalist for Best Juvenile Mystery, set in Berkeley, CA, featuring Skeleton Man who lives in a supposedly haunted house…

Book #2 - THE CODE BUSTERS CLUB: THE HAUNTED LIGHTHOUSE
Winner of the Agatha Award Winner for Best Juvenile Mystery, set on Alcatraz, featuring a jewel thief who stole—and hid—diamonds…

Book #3 - THE CODE BUSTERS CLUB: MYSTERY OF THE PIRATE'S TREASURE
Agatha Award Finalist and an Anthony Award Finalist, set at the Carmel Mission where California's only pirate robbed from the missionaries, who eventually hid their treasures—and then forgot where they were…

Book #4 - THE CODE BUSTERS CLUB: THE MUMMY'S CURSE
Agatha Award Winner, set at an Egyptian Museum, where a mummy may or may not come back to life, while the kids solve Hieroglyphic codes…

Book #5 – THE CODE BUSTERS CLUB: HUNT FOR THE MISSING SPY
Set at the International Spy Museum in Washington DC, where the kids explore the museums while being followed by a mysterious spy…

Coming soon: Book #6 – CODE BUSTERS CLUB: SECRET OF THE PUZZLE BOX

Join the Code Busters Club!

Visit the official CODE BUSTERS CLUB website at www.codebustersclub.com and join the club! Just fill out the information to receive your packet of code-busting supplies!

Top Secret Answers to the Coded Messages

Codes by the Code Buster Club kids

(Cody: My mom is teaching me police codes.)
(Quinn: The pigpen code looks like tic-tac-toe.)
(M.E.: The Mexican flag is code for hope (green), harmony (white), and heroes (red).)
(Luke: Write a message by mixing up the letters of each word. It's fun and easy! Code Busters Rule!)

Codes to Solve

1. Alpha-Numeric Code
 (Answer: You can also write the numbers in reverse.)

2. American Sign Language
 (Answer: Use the Sign Language alphabet to talk in secret.)

3. Braille Alphabet
 (Answer: Braille is used by blind people)

4. Caesar's Cipher
(Answer: The Caesar cipher wheel is fun to use!)

5. Egyptian Hieroglyphic Code
(Answer: Draw pictures to spell a message.)

6. Flag Code
 (Answer: Make your own flags to use for codes)

7. Phonetic Alphabet Code
 (Answer: Phonetic Alphabet Code is used in military.)

8. Pigpen Code
 (Answer: The pigpen code was used during the American Civil War.)

9. Pirate Code
 (Answer: Hey, Friend! Watch out for the bad guy who's been stealing loot and food. We'll punish the crazy thief by sending him to the bottom of the sea. Be quiet and good luck!)

10. Reverse Alphabet Code
(Answer: The reverse alphabet is one of the easiest codes.)

11. Semaphore Code
 (Answer: Send a semaphore message from across the playground.)

12. Texting Code
(Answer: Hey, Best Friend Forever! What's up, girl? See you later 4 whatev. Laugh out loud. By for now. Hugs and Kisses.)

13. Vowel-less Code
 (Answer: Sound out the letters to crack the code.)

The Code Busters Top Secret Codes

1. Alpha-Numeric Code

Write the letters of the alphabet. Underneath each letter, write a number, in sequence.

1 2 3 4 5 6 7 8 9 10 11 12 13
a b c d e f g h i j   k   l   m

14 15 16 17 18 19 20 21 22 23 24 25 26
 n   o   p   q   r   s   t   u   v   w   x   y   z

2. American Sign Language

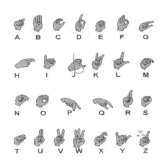

3. Braille Alphabet

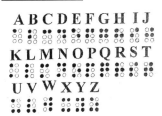

4. Egyptian Hieroglyphic Code

5. Flag Code

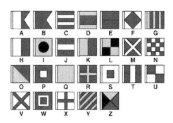

6. LEET Code

A = 4	B = 8	C = (	D = ｜)
E = 3	F = ｜=	G = 6	H = #
I = !	J = _]	K = ｜<	L = ｜_
M = M	N = N	O = 0	P = ｜*
Q = (,)	R= ｜2	S = $	T = +
U = (_)	V = V	W = W	X = *
	Y = \\|/	Z = 2	

7. Phonetic Alphabet Code

A – Alpha	J – Juliet	S – Sierra
B – Bravo	K – Kilo	T – Tango
C – Charlie	L – Lima	U – Uniform
D – Delta	M – Mike	V – Victor
E – Echo	N – Nov.	W – Whiskey
F – Foxtrot	O – Oscar	X – X-ray
G – Golf	P – Papa	Y – Yankee
H – Hotel	Q – Quebec	Z – Zulu
I – India	R - Romeo	

8. Pigpen Code

9. Pirate Code

10. Reverse Alphabet Code

Write the alphabet, then write the alphabet backwards underneath.

z y x w v u t s r q p o n m
a b c d e f g h i j k l m n

l k j i h g f e d c b a
o p q r s t u v w x y z

11. Semaphore Code

12. Telephone Code

A = .2	B = 2	C = 2.
D = .3	E = 3	F = 3.
G = .4	H = 4	I = 4.
J = .5	K = 5	L = 5.
M = .6	N = 6	O = 6.
P = .7	Q/R = 7	S = 7.
T = .8	U = 8	V = 8.
W = .9	X/Y = 9	Z = 9.

13. Texting Code

14. Vowel-less Code

Write the message, then remove all the vowels and run the letters together. Sound out the syllables until they make sense.

Example: MTTTHLBRRT1900HRS

15. Washington Code

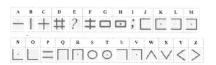

Create your own secret code below:

A
B
C
D
E
F
G
H
I
J
K
L
M
N
O
P
Q
R
S
T
U
V
W
X
Y
Z

How to make a Caesar Cipher

To make a cipher wheel:
1. Cut out the cipher wheel templates.
2. Put the smaller wheel on top of the larger wheel.
3. Insert a brad through the center of the smaller circle, then through the larger circle.
4. Spin the inner circle around so the letters on it will line up with letters on the outer circle.
5. To send and receive a message, decide on a 'key letter' that will be used to set the wheel.

To code a message:
1. First, write out your message on a piece of paper.
2. Twist the inner wheel until the key letter lines up with the letter A on the outer wheel.
3. For each letter in your message, find the letter on the outside wheel, then write the corresponding letter on the inner wheel in your coded message.

To decode a message:
1. Set the wheel so the key letter on the inner circle lines up with letter A on the outer circle.
2. For each letter in the ciphered message, find the letter on the inner wheel. Find the corresponding letter on the outer wheel and you will have the plaintext letter.
3. Write the plain text message on another piece of paper.

Author Penny Warner – Code Name: GRL SLTH

Made in the USA
Columbia, SC
13 May 2019